# Maci Masaki
## Makes Her Mark

## Charley Pickle

An imprint of Enslow Publishing

# WEST 44 BOOKS™

**WE THE WEIRDOS**

Amy Price for President!

What's the Matter with Jayden Jackson?

Maci Masaki Makes Her Mark

Eli Michaels, Rule Breaker

**Please visit our website, www.west44books.com. For a free color catalog of all our high-quality books, call toll free 1-800-542-2595 or fax 1-877-542-2596.**

**Cataloging-in-Publication Data**

Names: Pickle, Charley.
Title: Maci Masaki makes her mark / Charley Pickle.
Description: New York : West 44, 2020. | Series: We the weirdos
Identifiers: ISBN 9781538382073 (pbk.) | ISBN 9781538382080 (library bound) | ISBN 9781538383049 (ebook)
Subjects: LCSH: Friendship--Juvenile fiction. | Schools--Juvenile fiction. | Drawing--Technique--Juvenile fiction.
Classification: LCC PZ7.P535 Ma 2020 | DDC [F]--dc23

First Edition

Published in 2020 by
Enslow Publishing
111 East 14th Street, Suite 349
New York, NY 10003

Copyright © 2020 Enslow Publishing

Editor: Theresa Emminizer
Designer: Sam DeMartin
Interior Layout: Rachel Rising

Photo credits: Cover, p. 4 (Maci Masaki) Plattform/Getty Images; Cover ( cupcake, donut, rainbow, diamond) gst/Shutterstock.com; Cover (seahorse) wenchiawang/Shutterstock.com; pp. 1, 7, 16, 23, 30, 36, 43, 47, 51 (sea turtle) © istockphoto.com/Drawlab19; p. 3 (Amy Price) Digital Vision/Photodisc/Getty Images; p. 3 (Jayden Jackson) Arthur Dries/The Image Bank/Getty Images; p. 4 (Eli Michaels) Juanmonino/E+/Getty Images; p. 4 AllNikArt/Shutterstock.com; p. 7 Evgeniy Yatskov/Shutterstock.com; pp. 8, 56, 58 hchjjl/Shutterstock.com; p.14 Christopher Hall/Shutterstock.com; p. 16 NikonMaelao Production/Shutterstock.com; pp. 21, 46 LHF Graphics/Shutterstock.com; p. 24 frescomovie/Shutterstock.com; p. 28 lineartestpilot/Shutterstock.com; p. 29 Maria Averburg/Shutterstock.com; p. 33 hudhud94/Shutterstock.com; p. 36 wasa kong/Shutterstock.com; p. 40 silm/Shutterstock.com; p.44 Yuliya Serebrennikova/Shutterstock.com; p. 48 doodleboards/Shutterstock.com; p. 50 wenchiawang/Shutterstock.com; p. 52 puruan/Shutterstock.com.

Printed in the United States of America

CPSIA compliance information: Batch #CS18W44: For further information contact West 44 Press, New York, New York at 1-800-542-2595.

## Amy Price

**Clubs and Activities:**
Class President

**Most Likely to Be**
President of the
United States

**Quote:** "When life
hands you a lemon,
take the lemon and
run with it!"

*Amy Price*

## Jayden Jackson

**Clubs and Activities:**
—

**Most Likely to**
Win a Fight

**Quote:** "Get out of
my face, dude."

JAYDEN JACKSON

## Eli Michaels

**Clubs and Activities:** choir, cooking club, Volunteer club

**Most Likely to Cheer You Up**

**Quote:** "Do the right thing, and the sun will always shine your way!"

ELI MICHAELS

## Maci Masaki

**Clubs and Activities:** Art club

**Most Likely to Become a Famous Artist**

**Quote:** "I wish life were in watercolor."

Maci Masaki

**weirdo**: an unusual or unique person who is often not accepted by a larger group

## CHAPTER ONE
## Annoying!

My father thinks I am messy. My mother thinks I don't have friends.

Both of my parents are right.

But I don't need a clean room. And I don't need friends.

My father is standing at my door right now.

"Good morning, Mitsuko." He bows to me. He calls me my Japanese name. It is too hard for Americans to pronounce. My Japanese name feels like the old me. The one who used to live in Tokyo. I used to be Mitsuko Masaki. Now, I'm

Maci Masaki. I live in New York. I am a whole new person.

But my dad doesn't understand this. He still treats me like we live in Japan. I bow back, but I don't look at him. I am drawing. And I don't want to bow anymore. It's annoying! If I am drawing, I don't want to talk. And if I live in America, I don't want to bow.

"Today is O-souji," he says.

I nod again. I know! O-souji is a Japanese holiday. Like spring

cleaning. I don't know why we moved here if we are just going to do all the same stuff.

He pauses. He is silent. I draw a big turtle. A character I made. Turtle Samantha. She has a turtle shell for her head. But her body is a blue

Japanese school uniform. I write "OMG" next to her shell face.

My father is not impressed by Turtle Samantha. He does not understand manga comics.

"Your room is a mess!" he says.

There are pens on the floor. The drawers are stuffed with markers. There are clumps of neon-colored clothes on my bed. My school bag slumps in the corner. "Mitsuko. You must organize. Your room reflects your mind. And your mind is messy!"

I don't listen. I draw the next frames of the comic. Turtle Samantha sticks out her tongue. Then she puts her head back into her shell.

Sometimes, I wish I were Turtle Samantha.

My father does not speak. He is looking at the half-empty box of Japanese candy open on the floor.

"Where is your other slipper?" he asks, pointing to the one slipper under my bed.

I look up. "Don't know."

He sighs, "You don't wear slippers in the house anymore?"

"No. It's stupid. Shoes aren't dirty."

He picks up one of my sneakers. Then crouches down to where I am drawing. I am leaning with my back up against the bed. "Mitsuko, look."

I just want to draw. Why do we have to talk?

"See this?" He points to a pink blotch on the shoe. "This is chewing gum."

I nod.

"See this?" He points to a little gray circle. "This is dirt."

"It looks like half of a moon to me. I like it!"

"Really?" He places the shoe down on

my drawing. It leaves a footprint all over Turtle Samantha.

*Stop!* I think. But I don't say anything. I draw a speech bubble. Turtle Samantha says, "Fine! Step on me. I don't care. MY SHELL IS MY HOME!"

"It is not a home. It is a mess. You are a mess!" my father says.

I don't say anything.

He smiles very faintly. "Your mother and I would like you to have tea with us this afternoon."

Oh no. This cannot be good.

"We have something to discuss with you."

The last time they did this, they told me we were moving from Tokyo to New York City. They didn't give me a choice. They said we would leave for the next school year. My friends cried when I told them. But my friend Nanae made a YouTube channel for me. She posts videos from my Tokyo school for me to watch. I don't need American friends.

"Come downstairs at 2:00 p.m.," he says.

"Okay." I nod.

When he leaves, I look at my room.

My room is not a mess. It is my studio. I will be just like Hayao Miyazaki one day. He is a manga artist. He makes movies. Beautiful movies of beautiful worlds that do not exist. When I see his drawings, I leave my lonely world. I love his world. I plan to send him my Turtle Samantha comic. I hope he will give me a job in his film company. I don't need to clean up. I don't need to make friends. All I need to do is draw. It is the only thing that matters.

## CHAPTER TWO
## Kicked Out!

Snow falls outside. The kettle is boiling on the stove. The house smells like warm rice. It is nearly time for tea.

Today is December 31. My parents have been cleaning our apartment since December 13. They have cleaned the bathroom. The shower. The kitchen. They

have washed the cushions of the couch. They have

cleaned their room. They have even cleaned the cleaning supplies!

Maybe this conversation is to say we are going to move back to Tokyo. Nanae would be so happy! I could return to my old school.

My clock flashes the time: 1:58 p.m. I hear the water pouring into the teapot.

At 2:00 p.m., I slide open my door. I see my mother and father at the table. They are kneeling. They are both wearing dark pants and dark shirts. My mother has red glasses. My father has no glasses. They are both looking at me. They look stern.

There is a violin on the table.

My violin. It used to be my mom's. When she was learning.

But I don't play.

I sit down. They bow.

They pour me tea.

I wish I were drawing.

My father starts, "I have talked to Mitsuko about her room."

My mother nods. "Good."

I don't want to have this talk again.

"Mitsuko, you cannot take these habits into the new year with you, " my father says.

My mother nods. "We also need to talk about your lack of friends."

My stomach churns. I want to be Turtle Samantha. I want to curl up inside my shell. I don't like talking. I only like art.

And Nanae. Because Nanae said that Miyazaki will love Turtle Samantha and will definitely make a film about her.

My parents' faces are very serious. My father says, "You have not joined any clubs or activities at your school. We picked this school because it is not just Japanese people. It is all sorts of people. New people. New friends. This is not Tokyo. You have to find new friends."

"I have friends," I say.

"Who?"

"A girl."

"Does she have a turtle head?" my mother asks.

"Yes."

"No, she is not your friend," my mother says. My mother pushes the violin across the table to me. "You will join the orchestra."

"What?"

Both my parents nod.

"I don't like violin."

"I didn't like violin for the first five years that I played it," my mother says. "But now it is the first thing I do on the weekend."

It's true. My mother practices the violin on Saturday mornings at 6:00 a.m. I don't think my parents think they are annoying. BUT THEY ARE.

My father nods. "We are requiring you to clean your room and join the orchestra. You need to organize your life. You need friends. It is not possible to live life alone. Cartoons are not friends."

Cartoons! Ha! My drawings are not cartoons. This is manga. Art. My father does not understand anything.

He continues, "You have not cleaned your room, so you no longer get to sleep in it. The things we love need to be cared for. Like bonsai trees. You cannot neglect them."

My father has my grandfather's bonsai tree. He wants to pass it on to me. But I am not interested in taking care of a miniature tree. I am not like him at all.

"Mitsuko, are you paying attention?" my father asks.

I nod. I wasn't. But I don't think I missed anything.

"So, you can have your bed back when you clean your room and join the orchestra."

Wait, what? Maybe I did miss something.

"We ask that you sleep on a cot outside of your room until you show us you can tend to your room," my mother says. "Organize your room. Clean it. Join the orchestra at your school. Make friends. And, then, you can have your room back."

I am shocked into silence.

I think about Turtle Samantha. She needs a

superpower.

She can turn annoying people into sand. Then they will just wash away into the ocean. My parents love the ocean. They would not mind being sand. Then they could clean the ocean!

Well, maybe I do not want them to be sand.

"We will have a meeting in one week to review your changes in lifestyle," my mother says. She hands me the violin case. "You will take this to school tomorrow."

I am not going to play the violin. I don't want to be in an orchestra.

My father walks to the closet. He gets out the tatami, the Japanese mattress. It is very low to the ground. He puts one pillow, a sheet, and a comforter on it. "Here."

He then pulls the doors to my room shut. He posts a sign that says in Japanese, "Closed until Cleaned."

( Closed until Cleaned )

Then my parents take the tea and clean it up. They are cleaning up everything. All the time. They are trying to clean me up. But I don't want to be reorganized.

I am not happy. I hate how the violin sounds. I hate how it feels. It leaves a mark on my neck. The boys at my old school made fun of me. Told me it looked like a kiss mark. Nanae stood up to them. She said they had pop haircuts. She called

them mushroom boys. They did not like this. Ha!
But Nanae is not here. Not one of my friends is
here. They are across oceans. MORE THAN
ANNOYING.

## CHAPTER Three
## Maybe I Am a Weirdo

I t is the first school day after break. I am very tired.

I am on the train to Public School 71. I am drawing Turtle Samantha turning a violin into sand. The speech bubble

says, "This is a warning! Anyone who annoys me will become grains of sand!"

I practice an evil laugh out loud.

A man on the train looks up from his cell phone. "Are you choking?"

"No." I smile. "I'm just practicing laughing."

He gives me a strange look. A lot of people give me strange looks. I used to think it was because I only wear bright clothing. Even my shoelaces are neon. But I don't think this is why people think I'm weird. I think it is my personality. I don't care. I don't need friends who are boring! I like Turtle Samantha because she's different from everyone else. She is not afraid to be unusual.

I get off the train and walk to P.S. 71. The front hallway smells of bleach. Window cleaner. Lemons. Is the school doing O-souji too? I did not know Americans cleaned over New Year's. But they must. Everything looks very clean. The floors. The lockers. The lunchroom. I am shocked. I thought Americans didn't care about cleaning at all.

I put my coat and backpack in my locker. I have to carry my violin around the entire day. I cannot wait until lunch. I like to sit under my lunch table. It is very quiet there. And no one talks to me. I don't think they even know I am there. I will hide the violin under the table with me.

My morning classes are boring. I hate Life Sciences. The only class I like is art. In art, the teacher has changed the tables. We have new seats. I sit next to Amy Price. She sits at my lunch table. People say our lunch table is for weirdos.

I lug my violin case to the new seat.

"Need any help?" Amy helps me store the violin under my chair.

I nod. "Thank you."

"Absolutely!" she says.

Amy is so cheery. And confident. She is THE Amy Price. She won the class election. I voted for her. Amy has a stutter, so she sang her speech. Her singing was great! She is so funny. I would never want to sing in front of people. I would be too scared. Amy seems like she is not afraid of anything.

"Does *Konnichiwa* mean hello?" she asks me.

I am shocked. Amy knows Japanese?

"Yes," I nod. "You know Japanese?"

She smiles. "Not really. I just listen to a Japanese band while I run. And I know you're from Japan. So I thought I'd try it out. I thought it might have been something weird, like 'howdy partner.' But, I guess not." She is laughing, but I don't understand the joke.

"Howdy?" I ask.

"Oh, it's just what cowboys say!" She is smiling at me.

But I am still surprised that she listens to a Japanese band. Also, that she runs. What can't she do?

"You're a runner?" I ask her.

"I joined the track club. Ms. Shelby, the Life Sciences teacher, invited me. And it's cool. It's not like my old school, but still cool."

I did not know she is a new student, too. I guess I do not know much about this school.

The art teacher, Ms. Redford-Martin, tells us that we are making cloud sculptures today. We are hanging cotton from wires so the whole art room will have a cloud sky. She is smiling. She is holding a tree branch. I think the art teacher looks a little weird. She has long gray hair and always wears clothing with rainbows on it. Some people call her Ms. Rainbow-Magic to be mean. But I like Ms. Redford-Martin. She never says, "We can't do that" or "I can't do that." She says, "I'll figure it out." I think she used to be part of the circus. She is always drawing circuses.

At the end of class, Amy looks at my

sculpture. "Wow! Your clouds are beautiful. You did so many!"

I am so focused. I did not even realize.

Sometimes when I am making art, I forget about time. I say, "It is three types of clouds: rain, storm, and flat."

"OMG. Radical bananas!" Amy says. "You are so creative."

I don't understand this expression, "radical bananas." Maybe it is like "cool beans." Eli at the lunch table says this. I want to learn these expressions so I can fit in.

"Are you in comic club?" Amy asks.

"Comic club?" I ask. I don't know about comic club. Amy Price knows everything about this school! "No." I shake my head.

"You should join!" She pulls up a web page on her phone. There is a whole P.S. 71 website. I didn't even know about this. "Here, I'll send this to you. What's your phone number?"

A second after I give her my number, I get a text with the link. I am shocked again. I didn't know any of this was happening. I guess because I was always under the table. Maybe this is why most people don't eat their lunch under the table.

The website for comic club says they meet every Tuesday. They are having a contest for the school mural. The entries for the contest are due tomorrow. There is a link to submit them. The club will vote at the next meeting. This club seems cute. I want to go. Maybe I will join this club.

Maybe I can show them Turtle Samantha.

## CHAPTER FOUR
# Above the Table

The lunchroom looks totally different. The walls in the cafeteria look fresh. They are all white. The school must have taken off all the old posters that used to be there.

After morning classes, I take my lunch box and sit under the far table in the cafeteria. It is a great spot. From here, I have a good view of the fish tank on the wall. I like to draw Turtle Samantha under the table. I eat my lunch very quickly. The floor of the cafeteria is not clean, so I sit on my coat. My parents do not know I sit under the table. They would not be happy about this.

I made a movie for Nanae on my phone from under the table. She said that it was a very good video. She said that the kids who sit above the table were funny. But too bad they were above the table! I think she wants me to sit above the table.

These are the people who sit above the table:

**1**. One girl: Amy Price.

Amy is really different from my Tokyo friends. She is really confident. She has a calendar. She records notes for herself out loud on a recorder. Sometimes, I hear her and Eli sing together. I like the way they sing.

**2**. Two boys: Jayden and Eli.
Jayden was very angry for a while. He never talked

to anyone. I used to see his sneakers way at the other end of the table. But then he became friends with Eli. Now they sit together and talk about their band.

Today, the above-table kids are talking about Jayden and Eli's band.

"I wish I had a guitar," Jayden says. "I hate these bucket drums."

I feel bad for Jayden. He never seems to have the things he needs. I look at my violin case. I am carrying it around because it won't fit in my locker. It's so annoying. I get an idea. But the idea requires me to go above the table. I don't know if I want to do this.

So, I just take my violin and slide it up to the seats.

"What the…?" Jayden says, as he pulls the violin up on the table.

He takes the case and opens it. "A violin?"

Jayden says. "Nifty."

I don't know what nifty means, but it sounds good. Maybe it is like "radical bananas."

Then Eli and Jayden duck their heads under the table. "Hey."

They stare at me.

I wave. Then I go back to drawing.

I don't have to have a violin anymore. Problem solved.

"Wait! Why are you handing us this violin?" Eli asks.

"I don't like it," I say.

They look like they need more of an answer. "You said you needed a guitar," I add.

"Yeah, but come on, man, you can't just give your violin away. This is mad expensive," Jayden says.

"And it's not a guitar," Eli says.

"Duh!" Jayden says. "But it's a string

instrument. AND it's not just a violin. It's a Suzuki. These are from Japan. They're awesome. This would be so cool. Could you teach me, Maci? I could just borrow it."

I think for a moment. Nanae would want me to teach Jayden. I nod.

"*Domo arigato!*" Jayden says.

I laugh. "You're welcome." They know more Japanese than I thought.

"Do a fist bump!" Eli says. He demonstrates a fist bump with Jayden.

I smile. "Okay. Weird, but okay."

"We're weird? You're the weirdo hanging out UNDER the lunch table."

"So..."

"Don't you want to have friends?" Jayden says.

I shrug. "Not really."

"Come on. We are the best people ever! Sit

up here with us," Eli says.

I think about this. I don't really want to talk, but it would be nice to have a better drawing surface. "Okay," I say.

I tell them everything I know about violin from my lessons.

"We're part of a band. We play in front

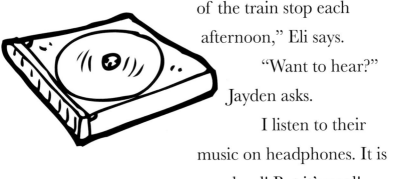

of the train stop each afternoon," Eli says.

"Want to hear?" Jayden asks.

I listen to their music on headphones. It is very loud! But it's cool!

"You should draw our album cover!" Jayden says.

Eli smiles. "We would be so cool then!"

"We're already cool," Jayden says.

"Not really," Eli says. "We are total weirdos."

Jayden laughs. "It's cool to be weird these days."

I nod. "That is so true."

"She knows! She's all neon!" Jayden says and points to my bright shoes and accessories. They don't match my uniform. I flush.

"No, those are dope, Maci," Jayden smiles. "Your style is fly!"

I smile. American expressions are very weird.

"So, what? You going to draw our album art?" Jayden says. "We can pay you."

I am embarrassed that Jayden brought up money. This is impolite to me. Americans talk about money a lot. But I think Jayden wants to compliment me, so I say, "Okay. Thank you! Yes. I would like to draw your music album."

Just like that, I have new friends.

## CHAPTER FIVE
# Radical Bananas

**O**n the train home from school, I decide I will join comic club. I really want to enter an idea for the mural contest.

That night, I draw for a long time at my kitchen table. I draw fourteen different ideas for the mural. At first, they have Turtle Samantha, but then she disappears. Instead, I start to draw Eli, Jayden, and Amy as fish. Then I draw other kids as fish. I draw them all in a big fish tank. A big tank of fish students. A school of fish. Many different fish swimming together.

I eat dinner with my parents. I don't tell them about today. I stay up drawing. I don't realize that it's 11:45 p.m. I scan my drawing and then send it.

The next day, I see Jayden, Eli, and Amy in the hall. Eli and Amy wave to me. I wave to Jayden. Maybe he is shyer than me. Maybe this school is not so bad anymore.

After school, I find comic club.

The school is very different after dismissal. There is the smell of popcorn. There is loud rap music. When I open the door, kids are laughing. They don't have their uniforms on anymore. One of them is standing on a chair.

I am so nervous. Maybe I should just walk out. They look like they are all friends. Maybe they are super-good artists. Or maybe they are horrible artists. Either way, I'm too scared to join right now. I'm about to leave, but a girl grabs my arm. In Japan, it would be so rude to grab a stranger's arm.

The girl says, "Hey, lady! Welcome to the monkey house!"

"Monkey house?" These American expressions are confusing.

"Oh, that's just what we call comic club." She points to a huge banner that says "MONKEY HOUSE" above the desks.

"Oh." I smile.

"I'm Audrey. What's your name?" she asks.

"Maci Masaki," I say. Sometimes it's weird to say my American name. But I think my Japanese name is too difficult.

"Cool. We are just about to vote on the mural design!" Audrey says.

"I sent one in, last night."

"Awesome!" she says.

Then she claps her hands and tells everyone, "Time for the vote!"

I take a seat.

Audrey shows each entry on the screen. We write our votes on ballots.

I'm not sure if we can vote for our own. I don't want to ask. I decide to vote for one that is a rainbow that blurs into raindrops. It is really good. Some of the others are really bad. I hope they don't win.

Audrey counts the votes. "Drum roll please!"

Everyone drums their hands on the tables. Some people make monkey noises.

Then Audrey says, "The winner is the new girl's fish tank!"

I wonder who this new girl is. I look around. Everyone is looking at me.

Then I realize, Audrey means me! The club chose my idea. I can't believe it!

A boy says, "You're a sick manga artist. You should quit school and write a graphic novel."

"I wish!" I say.

Audrey says, "Congratulations!"

Everyone claps for me. I can't believe it. This was much easier than I thought. I thought they would not like me. I did not know they would choose my work!

Audrey says, "For the mural, what if each student in the school wrote a message to go with their fish? Then everyone would be part of the mural?"

I nod. "This is a cute idea."

We spend the rest of the time drawing sketches of the different fish in the mural. I eat some of the popcorn. It is good. I feel like I am in an American movie!

Audrey says, "We are going to unveil this on February 18 for Parents' Night. They are going to love it! Can you stay after every day to work on it?"

"Totally!" I nod. I use an American expression I learned from Amy.

The other kids smile. "Cool!"

I try another Amy expression, "Radical bananas!"

They look at me, puzzled. "Is that a Japanese saying?"

I blush. I am so embarrassed!

I say, "No. I thought it was an American one."

Audrey laughs. "Nope! Just a weirdo one!"

We are all laughing. I guess my friends are weirdos. I don't care. I am just happy to have friends who told me about this club! I don't care if they are weirdos, because I am a weirdo, too! This is the first day of being twelve that hasn't felt annoying.

## CHAPTER SIX
# Organized!

**O**n the train home, I decide not to tell my parents about the mural. I want them to be surprised.

At home, my mom has made ramen. I love ramen. I miss the ramen shops from Tokyo. I went to one here. It wasn't the same. Nothing is the same.

"How was the first week back in school?" my dad asks.

"Good." I nod. I am slurping up a big noodle. After I finish chewing, I say, "I joined a club."

My mom looks up. She fixes her glasses on her nose and says, "Good. The orchestra?"

I do not tell them I gave away my violin.

"No, an art one. We study art," I say. I want my parents to think it is more serious than comics. They would not understand this.

"You are studying painters?" my dad asks.

"Pretty much." This is a very useful American saying. I don't have to be specific.

"Also, I have made three friends," I tell my mom.

My mom sets down her fork. "In the art history club?"

"No. At the lunch table. Amy, Jayden, and Eli. I am going to draw a picture for the boys. They are musicians."

My mother smiles, pleased. I think she is picturing classical musicians. I don't tell her they are in a metal band.

Also, I never told my parents that I sit under the table, so I don't think I need to tell them I sit above the table now.

My dad says, "We are proud of you."

"And tonight I will organize my room."

My dad's eyes shine with pride. "Yes! An ordered space is an ordered mind."

I nod. My parents offer me matcha ice cream for dessert. They are no longer angry. I cannot wait for them to come to Parents' Night and see my design. They will be so proud!

## CHAPTER Seven
## So What? I'm a Famous Artist.

**E**ach day after school, I work on the mural. In the second-to-last week of January, I draw each fish in pencil on the wall. It is fun. I am a real artist. I listen to music and draw alone in the cafeteria. Sometimes, people from the comic club come to help, but mostly it is just me. After I draw the fish, I begin to paint them.

One day at lunch, a girl and a boy admire my work. "Who did this?" they ask each other.

"It's Maci Masaki!" Eli says. "She is a very talented artist. Do you want her autograph?"

I am so embarrassed when Eli says this, but then the boy says, "Sure."

"Yeah, me too," the girl says.

I sign pieces of paper. I feel like I am a celebrity. I feel proud of myself when kids know me in the hall. More and more students tell me they like my fish mural.

The students smile and tell me they like the fish. They all want to know which fish will be theirs.

I tell Amy that her fish is going to be a shark. Jayden's is going to be a purple betta fish. Eli's is going to be an angelfish.

"Yes! Shark!" Amy says. "How did you know I like sharks?"

"You talked about them a lot before. When I

was under the table."

Amy laughs. "Wow, weird AND creepy!"

"Which fish are you?" Eli asks.

Jayden looks up from his lunch. "She is totally a neon tetra."

Eli laughs. "How do you know types of fish?"

"What, you think I'm not smart?" Jayden looks angry.

Eli blushes. "No, you're a genius for music. Not fish."

"I read a lot of hospital magazines when my mom's working. About a lot of things." Jayden's face softens. He laughs. "Including tropical fish."

Everyone laughs at this.

"We are all so weird!" Eli says. "Maci was sitting under the table! You and I are in a heavy metal band. Amy says weird words no one else says."

Amy laughs. "That's called being a poet. I was not weird at my old school."

"That's because your old school was a weirdo paradise!" Eli says.

Amy smiles. "Yes…but, still a paradise!" Then she looks up the neon tetra fish online.

"Maci is totally a neon tetra. You shine!" Amy shows me the picture of this small, bright blue fish. It has a red tail.

"Yes! I like the neon tetra!" I say. Actually, I love the neon tetra! I am so happy my friends think I am this fish.

After the week, I finish painting every fish. Our principal, Dr. Waters, got me sparkly paint. Stepping back from the mural, I see that it is beautiful. The fish swim all around the cafeteria. I take a lot of photos. I text them to Nanae. She texts back, "I love it. So cute. Now you are a famous artist. Maybe start a blog?" This is a great idea!

## CHAPTER EIGHT
# Digby the Disaster

The next morning, Amy sees me walk into school. She calls, "Maci!"

I turn. "*Konnichiwa!*"

But she doesn't say hello back. She looks serious. She says, "The mural is all messed up."

"What?"

"Digby Praxton wrote swear words in the boxes above the fish." Digby is the school bully.

"What?" I am shocked.

"Come see," Amy says. We walk into the cafeteria.

The mural has black marker all over it.
Digby wrote swears and insults in the speech

bubbles for the fish. He drew
crosses over their eyes to
make them look dead. I am
so angry. I want to go back
under the table. I just want
to draw for myself. I want to

be Turtle Samantha again.

I cannot hide it. I start to cry.

"It's okay," Amy says. She hugs me. "We can
fix it."

"How? Parents' Night is tomorrow after
school! There is so much damage. It will take me
days to fix it."

"I'm sure there's something we can do."

"I don't think so," I say, as more tears burn
my cheeks.

After school, I try to fix the marker. It does

not come off easily. I have to either paint the entire fish over or use a tiny brush to repaint the color over it. At 8:00 p.m., the maintenance worker tells me she needs to lock the school for the night.

At home, I slump on the table.

My father has made rice and shrimp, but I don't want to eat any of it.

"What's wrong?" he asks.

I decide to tell them the whole story. I tell them that art history club is really comic club. I tell them I submitted a design. I tell them it won. That I painted it. That a kid without a soul ruined it. And he didn't admit to it, so he didn't even get in trouble.

"The club selected your design?" my father asks.

"Yes."

"Wow. That is a true honor."

But I wanted them to see it at Parents' Night!

My phone rings. It's Amy Price. She is asking if she can come over.

"Right now?" I ask.

"Yes."

I ask my parents.

"It is too late."

I tell her that, but she says, "Well, actually I'm in your building's lobby with my mom and the other weirdos. We are waiting."

I tell my parents it is an emergency. They agree to let them up.

## CHAPTER NINE
# Friends and Chocolate

**W**hen my dad and mom open the door of our apartment, Amy introduces herself, her mom, Jayden, and Eli to my father and mother. My parents seems shy and embarrassed.

But Amy's mom takes her shoes off and puts on house slippers. She tells them about her visit to Japan for the Peace Corps.

"Really?" Their shoulders relax. They invite everyone in for tea. My mother sets out chocolate sticks.

"These are Japanese candy?" Eli asks, as he

takes another chocolate stick.

"Yeah," I say. "Do you know the song for the candy?"

"What? No!" Eli eats another.

I show him the commercial on my phone. He dances to it. "This is so cool! Jayden, we should play this song!"

I think he is on a sugar high.

Jayden nods. He is quiet around my family. Even shyer than me.

"Eli, don't get off track," Amy says. "We are on a mission."

My parents talk to Amy's mom in the kitchen. The weirdos and I gather around the kitchen table.

"So, I called Dr. Waters, and she said that

we can go into school tomorrow at 5:00 a.m. We can paint the mural before school starts. If we all work together, we can repaint it in time. Then it can dry during the day."

"Wow," I say. "Then it will be perfect for Parents' Night."

"Yes!" Amy says.

I say, "Radical banana!"

Amy Price laughs. This is the first time I said a joke and she laughed!

Eli has eaten all of the chocolate sticks. He is zooming around the kitchen.

Amy puts her shoes back on. "Come on, guys. We have to go. See you at 5:00 a.m. in front of the school!"

After my friends leave, my mother and father say goodbye to Amy's mom. They each put a hand on my shoulders. "You have made very kind friends, Amy. This is a hard thing to do."

I nod. "And you guys have made your first American friend. Who is not a business friend!"

My father blushes. He is embarrassed that I am speaking to him like this. He is so much older than me. But I know he knows this is true.

I lie in my own bed, in my neat and organized room. And for the first time since moving here, I feel confident.

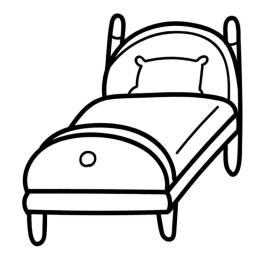

## CHAPTER TEN
# Parents and Weirdos

**W**e wake up so early. We paint over the marker. Each student writes a reason they are thankful to go to P.S. 71 in their bubble.

At Parents' Night, the mural is beautiful. The room smells like warm sugar cookies. My parents hold little cups of orange juice. They stand behind me looking at the neon tetra. It is bright blue. I used red sparkling paint for the tail. It is looking at the shark, the angelfish, and the betta. It says, "I'm in a new ocean. But I am happy for my friends at P.S. 71!"

My parents ask to take my photo in front of it. After, they ask to take a photo of all of my

American friends. When my dad counts down the photo, we shout, "Weirdos!"

At the end of the night, we ask our parents to sit with us at the weirdo table. My father sits next to Eli's mom, Pastor Kim. My mother sits next to Amy's mom. I hear them making plans to have coffee together. I sit next to Jayden's little sisters. They ask me to teach them how to draw horses. I do. Jayden's mom combs his hair. Jayden says, "Yo, Mom! Cool it with the annoying!" I am happy to know Jayden thinks his parents are annoying, too.

My parents look at me across the table. They are no longer nervous talking in English to Americans. I guess friendship doesn't require each person to be the same. Maybe friendships happen when people are different from one another. Maybe the things we like about each other aren't being from the same country, or looking the same, or speaking the same. But maybe a weirder thing.

We need friends who accept and see us for who we really are: weird, unusual, messy, unsure, not confident, but trying. Swimming along. Together. Maybe this is the most beautiful thing of all.

# Want to Keep Reading?

Turn the page for a sneak peek at
the next book in the series.

ISBN: 9781538382097

# CHAPTER ONE
## Tryouts!

The field smells like fresh-cut grass. Today is the start of the second week of football tryouts.

I am all steam and power. I am a guy in motion. My feet move up, up, up. Then to the right, to the right, to the right. To the left, to the left, to the left. Then grapevine, back and forth across the grass. I'm not the fastest kid. I'm not the strongest. I'm not the best thrower. But I'm doing okay.

My breath makes cloudlike puffs in the chilly

morning air. The sun bounces off the windows of my school. This is Public School 71 in the spring.

I'm wearing a practice jersey. By the end of this week, I want a real one. A Panthers jersey with the name "Michaels" and the number nine on the back. I really want to be number nine.

When I came into school this morning, I saw my name, "Eli Michaels," written on the comeback list. Eight guys got cut last week.

Today at tryouts, I have nervous, happy energy. I already made it through one round of cuts. If I get in, I can practice with the team all summer. Then we can be champions next year!

A lot of kids at my school think I'm a goody two-shoes. They think I always follow the rules because my mom is a pastor. I do think rules are important, but I don't think I'm a goody two-shoes. I want to play football just like the other guys. That'll show them I'm no angel.

# ABOUT THE AUTHOR

Charley Pickle holds
an MFA and is a published
poet and short fiction author.
In sixth grade, Pickle wore a historically
accurate Shakespeare costume to school on
Halloween. Sadly, no one else dressed up.
Feeling rather pathetic, Pickle quickly changed
into inspirational Shaquille O'Neal gym clothes.
Charley Pickle definitely knows what it's like
to be a weirdo and often seeks weirdo friends,
as they usually have tremendously good
senses of humor. Pickle can
be found on Twitter at
@charley_pickle.

Check out more books at:

www.west44books.com

An imprint of Enslow Publishing

WEST 44 BOOKS™